Let's Pretend

The Sound of PR

By Cynthia Klingel and Robert B. Noyed

The Child's World®

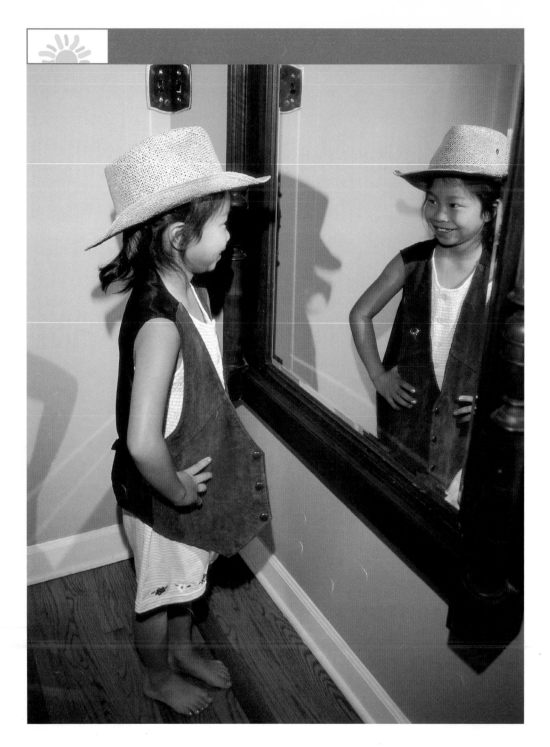

I like to pretend when
I play.

I pretend that I am
a princess.

I pretend that I win
a prize.

I pretend that I am
the president.

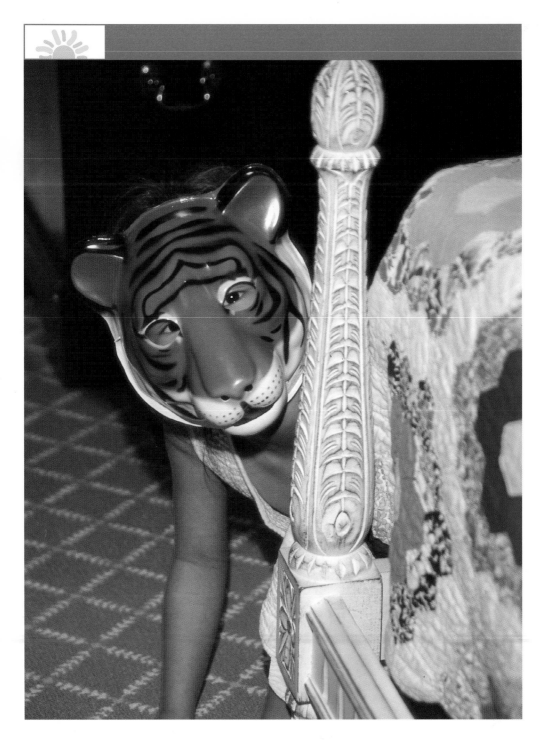

I pretend that I prowl like a tiger.

I pretend that I have many pretty dresses.

13

I pretend that I meet a prince.

I pretend that I work at the press.

I pretend that I prance like a dancer.

I can be many things
when I pretend!

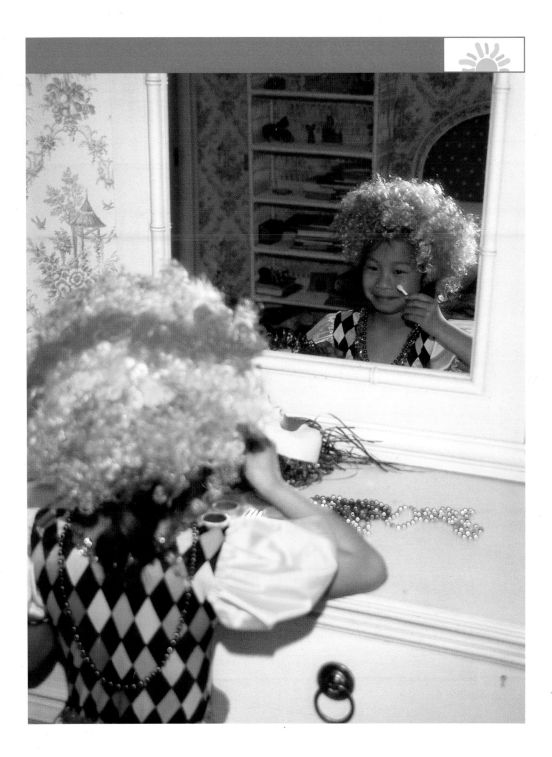

Word List

prairie	pretty
prance	prince
president	princess
press	prize
pretend	prowl

Note to Parents and Educators

Welcome to Wonder Books® Phonics Readers! These books are based on current research that supports the idea that our brains detect patterns rather than apply rules. This means that children learn to read more easily when they are taught the familiar spelling patterns found in English. As children progress in their reading, they can use these spelling patterns to figure out more complex words.

The Phonics Readers texts provide the opportunity to practice and apply knowledge of the sounds in natural language. The ten books on the long and short vowels introduce the sounds using familiar onsets and *rimes*, or spelling patterns, for reinforcement. The letter(s) before the vowel in a word are considered the onset. Changing the onset allows the consonant books in the series to maintain the practice and reinforcement of the rimes. The repeated use of a word or phrase reinforces the target sound. The twenty-one consonants and eight blends ("ch," "br," etc.) also use the onset-and-rimes technique.

As an example, the word "cat" might be used to present the short "a" sound, with the letter "c" being the onset and "–at" being the rime. This approach provides practice and reinforcement for the short "a" sound, since there are many familiar words with the "–at" rime.

The number on the spine of each book facilitates arranging the books in the order in which the sounds are learned. The books can also be arranged into groups of long vowels, short vowels, consonants, and blends. All the books in each grouping have their numbers printed in the same color on the spine. The books can be grouped and regrouped easily and quickly, depending on the teacher's needs.

The stories and accompanying photographs in this series are based on time-honored concepts in children's literature: Well-written, engaging texts and colorful, high-quality photographs combine to produce books that children want to read again and again.

Dr. Peg Ballard
Minnesota State University, Mankato, MN

About the Authors

Cynthia Klingel has worked as a high school English teacher and an elementary school teacher. She is currently the curriculum director for a Minnesota school district. Cynthia lives with her family in Mankato, Minnesota.

Robert B. Noyed started his career as a newspaper reporter. Since then, he has worked in school communications and public relations at the state and national level. Robert lives with his family in Brooklyn Center, Minnesota.

23

Published by The Child's World®

PO Box 326
Chanhassen, MN 55317-0326
800-599-READ
www.childsworld.com

With special thanks to the Jiganti and Knowles families
for supplying the modeling and location for this book.

Photo Credits
All photos © Romie Flanagan

Project Coordination: Editorial Directions, Inc.
Photo Research: Alice K. Flanagan

Library of Congress Cataloging-in-Publication Data
Klingel, Cynthia Fitterer.
Let's pretend : the sound of "pr" / by Cynthia Klingel and Robert B. Noyed.
    p. cm. — (Wonder books)
Summary: Simple text about pretending and repetition of the letters "pr"
help readers learn how to use this sound.
ISBN 1-56766-067-3 (lib. binding : alk. paper)
[1. Imagination—Fiction. 2. Alphabet.] I. Noyed, Robert B. II. Title.
III. Series.
PZ7.K6798 Le 2002
[E]—dc21
                        2001007814